AF559677

Birbal Goes to Persia

Books by Delshad Karanjia

Teaching a Horse to Sing: Tales of Uncommon Sense from India and Elsewhere
Akbar and Birbal: The Finest Stories of the Emperor and His Wise Minister

Birbal Goes to Persia

FOUR TALES OF AKBAR AND BIRBAL

DELSHAD KARANJIA

Illustrations by Mohit Suneja

ALEPH

ALEPH BOOK COMPANY
An independent publishing firm
promoted by ***Rupa Publications India***

First published in India in 2025
by Aleph Book Company
7/16 Ansari Road, Daryaganj
New Delhi 110 002

This is a work of fiction. Names, characters, places, and incidents are either the product of the author's imagination or are used fictitiously and any resemblance to any actual persons, living or dead, events, or locales is entirely coincidental.

ISBN: 978-93-6523-549-4

1 3 5 7 9 10 8 6 4 2

Printed in India

A Lesson for the Emperor

At an age when most men toil day and night to support their families, Akbar found himself at the helm of one of the greatest empires of the period. He lived a maharaja's existence in a luxurious palace with magnificent gardens, attended to by a retinue of loyal servants, surrounded by kowtowing courtiers who revered him as if he were a deity. Having

already been blessed so much by God, the young sovereign became obsessed with collecting material things—jewellery, art, Persian carpets, Arabian horses—anything his heart desired and that money could buy. Things were getting so out of hand that Birbal decided that it was time for the mighty emperor to face a few home truths.

One evening, as the emperor was heading back to the palace after a leisurely stroll through its magnificent gardens adorned with a hundred fountains and abloom with colourful and fragrant flowers, he noticed a sadhu who appeared to be fast asleep on the floor of a gazebo. Wondering how the man had entered the palace grounds, and making a mental note to have his guards punished for this trespass, Akbar walked over to the sadhu and nudged him with the tip of his pearl-embedded velvet slipper.

'Hey, you,' Akbar exclaimed. 'What are you doing here? This is private property; so get out of here immediately!'

Sitting up slowly and rubbing his eyes,

the sadhu adjusted his turban and asked: 'Huzoor, is this your garden?'

'Yes, it is,' said the emperor. 'This garden, the rose bushes, the jasmine, the mogras, the champaks, the fountains beyond that, the courtyard, the palace, the staff quarters, the stables, they all belong to me!'

The sadhu, whose face was almost completely hidden by the end of his turban and a thick white beard, stood up slowly. 'What about the river, huzoor? And the city, the country, the empire? Do they all belong to you?'

'Yes they do. They are mine, all mine. I order you to leave immediately!'

'I see,' said the sadhu, giving no

indication of leaving. 'And before you, huzoor, who did the palace and the garden and the city belong to?'

'Everything belonged to my father, of course,' the emperor replied, becoming a bit impatient at the man's persistence. Despite his dishevelled appearance, the sadhu appeared to be a learned man, and Akbar was admittedly intrigued by his questions.

'And who was there before your father?' the sadhu asked.

'My father's father.'

'Oh, I see. So the flowers, the fountains, the palace only belong to you during your lifetime. Before that they belonged to your father, and in years to come they will belong to your son, and then to your son's son?'

'Yes,' Emperor Akbar replied, wondering at this line of questioning.

'So each one is only temporarily in possession of all these things, is that right?'

'That is correct,' Akbar replied slowly.

'In that case, aren't you merely a custodian?' the sadhu continued. 'Everything you own is transitory. Someone took care of it before you and someone will always be there after you have gone. Is that not so?'

'It is,' the emperor said softly.

'Your garden, your palace, your city, your empire...these are only places you will stay in for a short while, for the span of your lifetime. When you die, they will no longer belong to you. You will depart, leaving them in the possession of someone else, just as your father and grandfather did.'

Emperor Akbar, stroking his chin, considered this revelation. 'I see what you are trying to explain to me: worldly possessions do not belong to a single person permanently, because each person is only passing through this earth and must die one day.'

The sadhu nodded solemnly. Then, bowing respectfully, he removed his white beard and saffron turban and said: 'Jahanpanah, please forgive me! I was only trying to get you to think about the transient nature of life. If you focus too much on material things, you may lose sight of the more meaningful things....'

'Birbal, dear Birbal! Thank you for teaching me a valuable lesson. Life is a journey, be it long or short. Everyone—whether prince or pauper—comes into this world empty-handed and must depart from it with nothing.'

'Most Blessed of Men do not get too attached to worldly possessions,' Birbal added. 'Instead, strive to be remembered for your good deeds. Let your actions become your monuments, built with memories instead of stone.'

Birbal and the Shah

The royal courts of Persia and Hindustan had shared close ties for several generations. In fact, shortly before Akbar's birth, his father Emperor Humayun had lost his throne after being defeated in battle by Sher Shah, founder of the Suri empire. The Mughal royal family fled to Persia accompanied by a few trusted friends, where they were given refuge by Shah Tahmasp. In exile for nearly fifteen years, Humayun eventually reclaimed the throne thanks to the help of his Persian allies and the military acumen of his army commander Bairam Khan.

When Akbar came to the throne, Shah Abbas, his counterpart in Persia, never let him forget the good turn his predecessors had done Humayun and his family. The shah patronizingly referred to Akbar as his 'younger brother' and went so far as to claim that Akbar owed his eminence to the magnanimity of his Persian benefactors.

Envious of Akbar, and keen to discover the secret of his success, widespread fame, and glory, Shah Abbas dispatched a letter to Akbar inviting him to send an emissary to Persia. He wrote:

> I have heard nothing but praise about your kingdom from my countrymen who have travelled its roads. I would like to learn more about your wondrous country from someone who has actually lived there.

Akbar promptly selected Birbal as his emissary. Preparations for the long and perilous journey began, and caravans loaded with gifts, precious stones, and treasures headed for Persia.

After weeks of travel by road and

by sea, Birbal arrived at the Persian king's opulent palace in Isfahan, with its magnificent and awe-inspiring architecture. Entering the grand hall with its high ceiling, tiled marble floor, and pillars encrusted with turquoise and gemstones that sparkled in the luminescence of a hundred candelabra, Birbal was surprised to see six identically dressed men seated on thrones on the dais at the end of the spacious room. Each of the men was elegantly dressed in splendid jewelled robes, all wore crowns, and all looked alike.

Realizing that he was being put to the test, Birbal looked from one to the other and then confidently strode up to one of

the men, bowed to him, and introduced himself, adding: 'It is an honour to be in your august presence, Your Majesty.'

'Birbal, the reports of your wisdom have not been exaggerated. How did you figure out that I am the king?' the puzzled monarch asked.

Birbal smiled: 'You were the only one of the six men who looked completely at ease on the throne. The five other kings looked self-conscious and kept glancing at you now and then. You alone looked as if you were to the manner born.'

The king of Persia was deeply impressed by Birbal's powers of observation. The visit was off to a promising start.

After a good night's rest, Birbal was ushered into the shah's presence the next day. 'Wazir Birbal,' the shah said, 'I am told that you are Akbar's most trusted adviser. Wherever I go, whoever I meet, everyone sings the praises of my younger brother, the great Akbar. What is the secret of his success?'

'His progressive thinking and humility,' Birbal replied confidently. 'He is wise enough to know that he doesn't have all the answers and humble enough to seek advice from those who do. Though he is surrounded by yes-men, he knows that minds are not stimulated by heads nodding in agreement. His greatest strength is that he bows to wisdom and never hesitates to seek guidance from his advisers.'

'That is indeed an admirable quality,' Shah Abbas said. 'I am deeply impressed by your candour and intelligence, Wazir Birbal. I know you have travelled far and have met many rajas and rulers, so I have one more question for you. Tell me, how do I compare with other kings?'

'Other kings may shine briefly but are unable to hold a candle to you. You are as majestic as the full moon.'

Suitably flattered, the shah smiled. 'And now you must tell me honestly, how do I compare with my younger brother, Emperor Akbar?'

'Emperor Akbar is the new moon,' Birbal replied.

Delighted with Birbal's response, the shah loaded him with gifts for his return journey. But news of Birbal's compliment to the shah had preceded him to Hindustan. Akbar was hurt and upset. Ignoring the piles of gifts from Isfahan, the emperor turned on his aide angrily and said: 'Birbal, you have betrayed and offended me! In open court you praised the shah of Persia as the full moon and compared me to the tiny sliver of a new moon?'

'Most Sublime Radiance,' Birbal replied calmly, 'what I meant was that, like the full moon, the shah's powers

will gradually wane, but like the crescent moon, you will continue to grow and glow until you reach your destined glory. You will be a shining light for years to come.'

With a laugh, Akbar embraced his friend. 'Welcome home, Birbal. I don't think anyone will be able to match your brilliance and sparkle. You outshine us all.'

Catching Thieves

Birbal had become so adept at solving petty crimes, that whenever a theft took place anywhere near the capital, the victims usually headed for Akbar's court rather than to the police to solve the case.

A rich merchant turned up at the durbar one day claiming that he had been robbed. His wife's jewellery and a bag of gold coins were missing and the merchant suspected that the theft had been carried out by one of his seven employees. Birbal accompanied the merchant to his house and questioned the employees, all of whom swore that they were innocent and denied any knowledge of the theft.

Birbal had anticipated their denial. 'I will give each of you a stick of equal length,' he told the seven men. 'These sticks have magical properties. By tomorrow morning when I come to inspect them, the thief's stick will have grown by two inches.'

The next morning, when Birbal inspected the sticks that he had handed out the day before, he found that one of them was two inches shorter than the others. Pointing to the employee with the shorter stick, Birbal said: 'This is your thief, merchant. The guilty man has cut the stick at night fearing it would grow by two inches.'

On another occasion, one of the emperor's ministers complained that his house had been robbed and all his gold coins had been stolen during the night. Akbar was shocked to hear about the theft because the area surrounding the palace, where all his ministers lived, was believed to be the safest in the kingdom. How could anyone have broken into the house at night to steal the coins? It could only be one of his ministers who had carried out the theft.

The emperor turned to Birbal to solve the case. Birbal asked for a cow to be tethered to the gate leading to the ministers' quarters. He told the puzzled ministers: 'This sacred cow has extraordinary powers. Each of you must lift its tail and loudly declare, "I did not steal the gold coins". If you are lying, the cow will moo loudly. Once you have undergone the test, please come straight back to the durbar.'

The ministers did as they were instructed and trooped into the durbar in the evening. When all of them were present, Birbal asked each one to hold out their hands, palms facing upwards so that he could inspect them. All the

men had streaks of black on their palms, except for the minister who had stolen the coins. Birbal had applied a semi-permanent dye onto the cow's tail knowing that the guilty party would not touch it, fearing he would be found out. He had managed to catch the thief using his usual unconventional methods.

A Tax on Fools

When not attending to affairs of state or waging wars to extend his empire, Akbar had a tendency to concoct bizarre assignments to keep his courtiers busy.

Thinking aloud, the emperor said to Birbal: 'I've come to realize that we have to bear the cost of other people's foolishness, while the fools get away without paying anything. It is most unfair that sensible people should have to pay the price for the stupidity of others. I think the only way to redress the balance is to initiate a tax on fools. In order to impose this tax, I will need a list of all the fools in my kingdom. Please start preparing the list right away.'

Birbal sighed and began drawing up the longlist of every fool in the empire. While he was preoccupied with this time-consuming challenge, a pearl trader from Bahrain stopped by at the royal court and was granted an audience with the emperor, who had a penchant for collecting precious gems from around the world.

From a pocket in his thobe, the trader fished out a small cloth bag containing pearls of various shapes, sizes, and colours. An oval pearl, the size of a quail's egg, caught the emperor's eye.

'O Most Discerning of Men,' the pearl trader began, 'you have picked out the most prized gem in my collection. If you hold this beauty up to the light you will see its subtle lustre and rarest of rare pink hues. I call this pearl Blushing Bride because of its glowing tint.'

'It is indeed an exquisite gem. I have never seen another like it,' the emperor said, turning the pearl around and admiring its beauty.

'O Jewel among Men,' the trader said,

'I have been diving for pearls for more than fifteen years and have a few more priceless gems identical to this one at my shop in Bahrain. If you are interested in adding them to your legendary collection of gems, I will consider it an honour to sell you ten of my largest pearls, this one included, for a hundred gold coins each. As I must make the long journey by road and sea to Bahrain and back, I would be grateful if full payment could be made to me in advance. You may keep the Blushing Bride, and I assure you that her nine equally stunning bridesmaids will be in your possession within the month.'

Akbar signalled to his treasurer to hand over a thousand gold coins to

the pearl trader, who was so overjoyed at receiving this bounty that he walked the entire length of the large durbar hall to the exit backwards, bowing all the way.

When Birbal heard about this impulsive transaction, he decided to speak to Akbar about it.

'Huzoor, is it true that you gave the Bahraini trader one thousand gold coins for ten pearls after seeing only one sample?'

'Birbal, you know I have a keen eye for jewellery and am something of an expert. The pink pearl he showed me was so exquisite, it will be one of the most prized gems in my collection. I think I struck a good deal with the trader today,' Akbar replied.

'Did anyone at court introduce this man or recommend him to you? Isn't it risky to trust someone who walks in off the street?'

'Birbal, unlike you, I am not suspicious of everyone I meet. I don't think people cheat you if you put your trust in them,' Akbar said, not noticing Birbal rolling his eyes in disbelief. 'And by the way, how is the register of fools coming along? Is it nearly ready?'

'It is almost ready, huzoor, I only have to add one name.'

The following day, Birbal presented a lengthy scroll to the emperor. Taking a while to unfurl the bulky parchment, the emperor was shocked to see the name Jalaluddin Muhammad Akbar heading the list of fools in the kingdom.

'What is the meaning of this, Birbal?' Akbar yelled. 'How dare you add my name to this list?'

'Most Revered Monarch, far be it from me to cause you any distress. But you have entrusted one thousand gold coins to an unknown person from a far-off land whom you don't know and may never see again. Isn't that foolish?'

Gritting his teeth, Akbar replied: 'The man has promised that he will be back within the month.'

'Well, if he does turn up, I will remove

your name from the list and replace it with his,' Birbal replied.

Suppressing a smile, Akbar said: 'On second thoughts, I think we should give up the idea to collect a tax from fools. Nobody will want to be assessed in that category.'

'That is a sensible decision, Exalted Leader,' Birbal replied. 'I think it would be easier and more beneficial for us to collect revenue if we call it a tax for the wise. Even the fools in your empire will be delighted to pay a wisdom tax.'

Akbar rubbed his chin and nodded as he considered Birbal's suggestion.

'If all the foolish people in the land come up with what they think are clever ways of avoiding the fools' tax, it will only make more work for us all,' continued his adviser. 'One should always be wary of fools who think they are too smart.'